A

Hitman's

Confessions

Written By: Yuanis Heathington

Copyright © 2023 by Yuanis Heathington

Published and Edited by: Kasir Entertainment

All rights reserved. No part of this book may be reproduced by any mechanical, photographic, electronic process or phonographic recording – other than for "fair use" as brief quotations embodied in articles and reviews without prior written permission of the publisher.

Yuanis Heathington

Printed in the United States of America

Dedication

As the narrator of this book I would like to dedicate this literary work to my Mother Liz and my children Yuanez, Kamren and Demarcko. You all mean so much to me and my only goal is to continue to make each of you proud!

Contents

Acknowledgements

Chapter 1 The Very Beginning

Chapter 2 Teenage Years

Chapter 3 Death Knocks Again

Chapter 4 The Killer in me is Awakening

Chapter 5 My Skills Will Be Tested

Chapter 6 Seasoned Veteran

Chapter 7 When Shit Hits the Fan

Chapter 8 Getting Back to Me

Chapter 9 Back to Business

Chapter 10 The End All Be All

Acknowledgements

I would like to give a special thanks to God for allowing me to discover my gift of writing during a time that was hard for me and also blessing me to overcome those challenges, so that I can continue to use all the gifts given to me. I would like to thank my beautiful mother Liz, my amazing children Yuanez, Kamren and Demarcko. I would thank my editor Rayesha Tenn. I would also like to thank my Brother Eric, my cousins James, Chin, Robert, my Frat brother M.O.B mu O. and all of my family and friends.

I would also like to acknowledge the person that this book is about for all of his stories and for allowing me to put his life in narration. Watch out for the movie to follow soon! Last but not least, I want to thank everyone who purchased a copy of this work! Thank you all tremendously!

A Hitman's Confessions

Chapter 1

The Very Beginning.

My childhood was just like any other childhood, very innocent. I grew up with my mom and stepfather in the home until a tragic incident occurred. On September 24, 1986 the feds raided our home and took my mom and my stepfather to jail for drug trafficking. My real father never had anything to do with me so I was forced to stay with my grandparents. Eventually, my mother was released from jail but left me at my grandparent's home until she recovered from the losses we suffered. In those days any property seized by the federal government became property of the government. My mother was a strong woman mentally and physically (as I would soon find out). The ultimate hustler, she was a go-getter for real. When the feds hit the house they found over 3 Kilos of powder cocaine and over a 100,000 in cash and just about the same in jewelry and clothes (Mink coats, Gucci Jogging Suits, etc.). My mother drove a 1986 E Class Mercedes Benz golden brown with black leather seats and gold BBS rims. My stepfather was the flashy type as well. He was a very muscular, dark skinned man with a head full of waves and gold chains everywhere. If he was to cut his hair into a Mohawk he would remind you of Mr. T. My stepfather was a very aggressive man who loves everyone but you bet not ever cross him.

    Prior to the raid, my life was a dream. I was a kid who could have anything I asked for. Whether it was kangaroo boots or a Max Julien coat to the latest Atari games. I was a spoiled brat of a child I must admit but just in a day all that changed. My stepfather took the rap for all the drugs and money to have the sentenced lowered for my mother. He received seventeen years while my mother received three years of which she only did a year and a

A Hitman's Confessions

half. Upon her release she totally changed her life around and was working to receive her license in real estate and had also started working for the City of Detroit. During the time that my mother was getting her life together I continued to be raised by my grandparents. My grandparents were beautiful people. My grandmother was a school administrator that didn't take no shit. While my grandfather was an Ex-Marine who served for over 21 years then retired and started doing construction. Where he would finally become a super wealthy man. My grandparents had 3 children together but as many men in that day, my grandfather had 18 other children with different mothers from his time away in different countries and different deployments. Yeah it was a tough situation for my grandma but she stuck by her husband (but don't get it twisted she made his ass pay in many different ways). Needless to say she got hers.

A Hitman's Confessions

Staying with my grandparents was fun for a while. I was taught a lot of interesting things. My grandfather was a manly man. We took many camping trips year after year. My grandfather taught me to fish, how to start a fire and most importantly how to hunt and kill animals. I remember my first kill. I was about thirteen years old and we were hunting deer's. At this point I had been hunting with my grandfather for years but this year in particular, my grandfather decided to allow me to shoot at the prey. I could vividly recall him handing me his 30/30 rifle with the scope on it. I remember the rifle felling super heavy in my hands and my heart racing uncontrollably. He told me to look through the scope and calmly take long, slow breaths. I guess he could see the nervousness. As I looked through the scope I saw a big buck with super huge Antilles. I could see the deer so clearly in this scope. I slowed down my breathing to match the breath of the deer around the tenth breath, then Bang! I pulled the trigger of the rifle and watched the blood splatter hit the tree behind the deer and the deer's body took two steps and fell over. I could hear my grandfather yell, "Boy you got that motherfucker! A clean head shot! That was a great shot grandson just down right magnificent! I'm going to start calling you dead eye that's your new name." This was the very first time I seen my granddad super excited and happy. My grandfather was so proud of me that day and from that day forward he would take me shooting many times after that. I guess in his mind he was preparing me for the military cause every time we would go shooting he would say, "You're going to be an army ranger or a navy seal. A super killer for the government." Needless to say after that first deer kill, I fell in love with the feeling of the kill.

    As the years rolled by I became more and more accurate with my shots. I really started learning the fundamentals of the weapons I was shooting and how to break them down and reassemble them as well. I learned how to oil the barrels and adjust the calibration of the barrel and scopes. I enjoyed spending this time with my granddad and he didn't say it but he enjoyed the time too. I could tell by the conversations we would have. During these times we wouldn't just shoot guns but he would also teach me all the elements of personal protection, whether it was with knives and machetes or hand to hand combat. It amazed me the level of expertise this mild mannered man had. He would justify it as letting the lion loose. When he let the lion loose he would become someone totally different. Brucie the Killer Lion was his alter ego. Now Brucie was a maniac and when he turned into Brucie he was a straight killer. I mean the stories he would tell me was crazy but amazing at the same time. I remember the first time he told me about his first kill in the war, boy was that a crazy story.

Chapter 2

Teenage Years

Turning sixteen was the highlight of my life but it was also the time I started to encounter death up close. I mean I've seen death but never a human only animals that I shot down during our hunting encounters. I loved school! Education was important to me. I was that student that excelled in all my classes and I was even deemed the class smart ass. I guess you could call me a nerd but one who had swag. I wasn't the typical nerd. I was an athlete playing two sports. I was the student council president and popular. I was popular so much so that I was asked to attend the senior prom by this beautiful senior named Tamika Reynolds. Tamika was super smart, with thick thighs and pretty legs. She stood 5'4, brown skinned about 135 pounds but not fat, a thick bodied young lady with a wonderful personality. I still remember the day like it was yesterday. I spent the early part of the day getting my tuxedo and flowers together for our date to her prom. I made sure to get my car washed and waxed (*yeah I was sixteen with a car, an 87 firebird to be exact*) and was ready for our date. I picked her up around 8pm and after about an hour of taking pictures, shaking hands and meeting family members we were ready to head to the prom.

  While driving, I noticed Tamika sitting in the passenger seat staring at me with a sexy look on her face. The words that came out of her mouth had me in a choke hold…"Boy you really look good in that tux. Makes me wanna…" Before I knew it, Tamika was unbuckling her seatbelt and then she started un-fastening my pants. "I'm going to give you head while you drive us," said Tamika. What was I supposed to say? I simply smirked and continued driving while she was giving me a blowjob and boy was she good at it. The more she sucked, the more I begin to lose focus and it started to become very difficult to drive. "Tamika… baby you gotta stop. I can't…" but before I could finish my sentence a car hit my front fender, spinning us around two or three times before we hit a telephone pole. Tamika was thrown out from the inside of the vehicle, and I hit the steering wheel head first before the airbag deployed, sending hard plastic and metal shavings in my face, arms and neck. All I could remember was some guys pulling me out from the vehicle. I had a terrible headache and there was blood everywhere. I asked about Tamika but no one seem to hear me. I begin to panic.

"Where the fuck is my girlfriend Tamika? Is she ok? Where is she?" I yelled. Finally, this young guy says to me.

"Bro, I think you should just worry about yourself. She isn't with us anymore. She's DEAD."

A Hitman's Confessions

I couldn't believe what I was hearing. *Was this all a dream? Was this truly happening to me?* "Dead? What do you mean dead? Where is she? I'm trying to find her!" I screamed. I finally reached where Tamika was laying, someone had covered her body and face with a coat off someone's back. My heartrate began to drop as I removed the coat off Tamika. "Oh my God! Tamika!" I cried out. I instantly became sick and started throwing up all over the ground as I stared at her lifeless body. Tamika head was cracked open and parts of her brain was hanging out with her eyes open but looking to the left. I was in a state of shock.

Before I knew it I was being tackled by the Detroit Police. Why they were tackling me I didn't know but I was bleeding from the accident still and this cop was laying on top of me, restraining me. I was still in shock after witnessing my girlfriend's brains on the ground. After about ten minutes the cops let up on me. I guess they got the story about what had happened and let me get back up to my feet. By this time I was dizzy and couldn't really stand. One of the officers said...

"Just relax the ambulance is on the way, just relax."

I was in disbelief at what this man was saying, thinking how could I relax.

"I need to call my mom. Please, I need to call my mom" I said.

"Don't worry she's already been notified and so has Tamika parents," said the officer.

I guess one of the onlookers knew Tamika and had already contacted her mom and dad, seeing as though we wasn't far from Tamika house, we had literally just left. By the time my mom arrived, the ambulance was pulling up at the same time. Tamika parents had also arrived at the scene and they were hysterical. They were fighting with the officers, trying to get pass the yellow tape that the cops had blocked the streets off with. Seeing the look of despair on

A Hitman's Confessions

their faces, made me feel even worse. I wanted to run to them and tell them how sorry I was but off to the hospital I went.

I stayed at the hospital for a few hours going through test after test. All of the wombs I had got bandaged up and there were no serious injuries, so they gave me a few prescriptions and let me go home. The next day or so I started to receive crazy phone calls with people saying they were going to kill me and then hanging up. I think I received about five or so calls before it dawned on me that it had to be someone from Tamika family. Someone wanted revenge but for what I didn't know. I decided to call Tamika parents and tell them the complete story about what happened with the accident and to find out about funeral arrangements. Tamika mom answered the phone and as she spoke, you could still hear the pain in her voice.

"Hello" she said.

A Hitman's Confessions

"Hello, Mrs. Reynolds this is Colt. I wanted to call and tell you what had happened." Before I could say another word she cut me off and started yelling at me.

"WHAT the Fuck are you calling here for? You killed my baby girl. I can't stand yo' ASS! Don't let me see you in the streets or you'll end up the same way!"

After about three or four minutes of threats from Mrs. Reynolds, Mr. Reynolds takes the phone from his wife and starts to talk to me. I could tell he was upset as well but she was beyond pissed. Mr. Reynolds gave me the information about the funeral arrangements but urged me not to attend seeing as though his wife was totally upset. Needless to say I wasn't able to attend the funeral. Mrs. Reynolds was dead set on it, so I decided to remember Tamika in my own way. I truly felt bad for what happened but I hated how the blame was being placed on me.

Everyone was tore up about the death of Tamika. People at school, her family for sure, and even niggas in her neighborhood. Tamika was really missed by everyone including myself. Since her family wouldn't allow me to attend the funeral, I decided to go to Belle Isle with my best friend to get drunk and grieve. Belle Isle was an island in the middle of the city where everyone would go to show off their cars, BBQ and just have a good time without harassment by the police. It was also a place that a lot of drama happened. When you mix drinking and a lot of people something was bound to happen. My best friend Dontae and I were parked on the strip, standing outside of his car drinking while I reminisced about the memories of my girlfriend who just passed because of my carelessness or was it really my carelessness? Tamika was the one who started the whole thing but I should have stopped her sooner. I was battling with my own conscience then out of the blue gunshots rang out and they sounded really close. Being at Belle Isle it was normal to hear gunshots but they brought me back to reality quickly. Looking around trying to locate where the shots were coming from, I saw Dontae laying on the ground on the side of his car. I hide behind the car to avoid the bullets while yelling for Dontae to come where I was so we could get the hell out of there somehow. Just so happens the police was close to the area and pulled up almost instantly and saw the shooter. While we were hiding the police was able to capture the suspect that had been shooting. At this point I made my way to the side of the car where Dontae was laying only to find out that my best friend had been shot in the head. A bullet hit him right between the eyes and once again death had crossed my door. In the matter of a week I had lost two of the most important people in my life, my girlfriend and my best friend.

    I started yelling for assistance and for someone to call the ambulance to help Dontae. The police who had caught the person shooting ran over to assist me with Dontae. I was told to back up and let them try to revive him but clearly he was dead. When I did back away from my friend's body I was able to see the person who had been caught by the police. The man was in the back of the police car. Low and behold the person was Tamika's older brother. Then it instantly dawned on me that those bullets were meant for me. I was the target and my best friend Dontae ended up dying because of me. Dontae caught bullets that were meant for me and once again, my heart was shattered. This messed with my mental for years. I blamed myself for many years for the deaths of my girlfriend and best friend. At some point it started to drive me crazy and turned my heart cold. Made sense though, I was only sixteen years old and had encountered death twice in a matter of a week and it seemed as if all fingers were being pointed towards me as the one to blame. Funny how life goes and how things can always take a sudden turn.

Chapter 3

Death Knocks Again

After losing my friends I was a mess inside. Tamika's family definitely wanted my head on a platter. Turns out that Dontae's mom didn't blame me but didn't want me around because the pain hurt so much she couldn't look at me. Tamika's brother Mike ended up getting second degree murder for shooting Dontae and I was still receiving threatening calls from her family every now and then. It had gotten so bad that my granddad bought a gun for me to walk around with. I know what you're saying he bought a gun for you at sixteen, yes he did. My granddad knew how good of a shooter I was and if someone was coming to take me out at least I had a chance to defend myself. His reasoning was that there were kids fighting overseas at my age so it was only right for me to be prepared for anything

A Hitman's Confessions

that may come my way. It was a week after my seventeenth birthday when another tragic event shook our world. This one would be the event that drove me over the edge as well as my family.

My sister at the time was seven years old and my sister, my mom and grandmother was visiting our great aunt at her house on 23rd street. This was the house that our family frequently visited so needless to say we knew everyone on the block. My sister was next door at the neighbor's house on the porch with the neighbor's daughter playing in the field between the neighbor house and my great aunt's house. My cousins were walking from the store with some guys from the neighborhood. My cousin called himself being a member of the neighborhood gang and they had problems with some dudes on the other side of the hood. Well on this particular day these dudes decided that they were going to come to my cousin's hood to get revenge for a fight they had at school a few weeks prior.

A Hitman's Confessions

They rode bikes into my cousin's side of the hood looking for any of the gang members. Just so happens they started riding down the street and seen my cousin and his homies walking back towards the house. This was their chance to get revenge, so they pulled out guns from under their shirts and started firing shots at my cousin and his homeboys. Everyone scattered, trying to duck the shots. My cousin who was running to take cover, ran on the porch of the neighbor house where my sister and her friend were playing. I don't know what he was thinking but the guys saw him run up on the porch and continued to shoot at him. They shot over twenty-six times and when it was all over, the only people that was hit were my little sister and the neighbor's daughter who was around the same age as my sister. My cousin wasn't touched except for bruises from him running through the screen door. My mother and grandmother who were next door heard the shots and went to investigate what had happened. My mom went ballistic when she found her daughter bleeding like crazy from the neck.

The police and medical crews were called immediately. Right after my grandmother called my grandpa, my uncles and myself. When I arrived to the scene my whole family was there. There was a lot of crying and cursing, guns everywhere and everyone was talking to my cousin the one who was being shot at. The conversation started becoming heated as I approached them.

"Why in the fuck did you run up there with yo' stupid ass!" I heard my uncle screaming.

"I don't know Unk," my cousin responded.

"It's a big ass field right next door you could have ran through but now my niece is gone because of you! You pussy ass punk! I should kill you!" said my uncle.

"I promise I wasn't thinking, I'm sorry." My cousin said.

A Hitman's Confessions

That was all I needed to hear. I was already crying and emotional and to find out it was my cousin fault made it worse. I lost it and ended up beating the brakes off my cousin that day. I fought him so hard I almost killed him with my bare hands. After about 15 minutes or so my uncles started pulling me off of him. "That's enough! That's enough! I know you're upset but you're going to kill him," one of my uncles stated. I didn't care if I had almost beat him to death, nothing mattered to me at that time. My feelings were all over the place. Yeah I had seen death twice before but not this close. My mother lost it and was so hysterical she didn't know the time or place at that moment. When the ambulance was picking up the bodies my mom was pacing back and forth talking to herself as if she couldn't believe what had just happened. My grandma was right behind her trying to reason with her but she was not listening. After a minute or so she just screamed with so much pain that I started to cry even more.

A Hitman's Confessions

  At that moment I could only imagine how bad my mom was feeling. It was true I had lost a sister but my mother had just lost a daughter, her baby girl at that. I tried to hug my mom but she refused to be held, even by me. My mom became so delirious that the medical staff had to give her a shot in her arm to calm her down. They threatened to take her to the medical ward but my grandma refused. They assured them that they would watch over her. Days after the shooting were even rougher than on the actual shooting day. My mom would just sit in her room on the side of her bed smoking cigarettes and rocking back and forth in her own world. She wasn't strong enough to handle the funeral arrangements so my grandparents made the arrangements and paid for them as well. During that time we didn't have any insurance to bury my sister but the family somehow came together to make it possible.

  The day of the funeral was a horrible day for me and my family. My mom was completely broken down as she walked into the church. My uncle had to pick her up off the ground and continue to hold her up as they approached the casket. "WHY? WHY GOD? WHY?" My mom yelled at the top of her lungs to the most high. I wept in sorrow because I couldn't help ease my mom's pain. My grandmother held me close to her chest and assured me my mom would be ok. "She has to get it out. She's going to be fine," my grandmother said. That calmed my spirit down a bit, until I seen that bitch ass cousin of mines. I tried to break away from my grandma but she must had sensed what I was thinking and she held me even tighter. "No, not in here. This is not the place," my grandmother said in my ear. Just as I was calming down, my mom got a look at my cousin bitch ass and went on a rampage trying to get at him. She was so aggressive my uncles who were all military men had trouble keeping her restrained. "I'ma kill you! You punk ass bitch!" My mom yelled at my cousin. It got so bad my cousin was force to leave the funeral for his own safety.

Chapter 4

The Killer in me is Awakening

After the death of my little sister. My mom became very depended on prescription drugs to cope with the pain. If you asked her about her daughter she would reply she has no daughter. Things got worse when there were no more prescription drugs and the doctors wouldn't give her anymore. The next option was for her to get the drugs off the street and that's when her life turned for the worst. My mom became really depended on the street drugs until she began to lose everything. I would leave for school in the morning and see my mom hanging on the corner looking for her next fix. Inside this really tore me up. As much as I tried to plead with her to stop it didn't matter because it was her way of escaping the pain. Parts of me understood it but I didn't like it but I did understand her pain because in

A Hitman's Confessions

my own right I was suffering as well. I was told that my cousin wanted to speak with me, I guess to try and clear his name with me or to apologize for his action or whatever. I didn't want to see him because I still had a lot of rage inside and even more now knowing that my mom was now on drugs. In my eyes he was the source to all my pain.

    Against my better judgement I eventually met with the cowardly ass nigga. I had my cousin meet me somewhere very private and desolate so if I did get upset and struck him no one would be able to witness my actions. We ended up meeting at the High School in the neighborhood. At this High School was a little cut right by the football field away from the street and very secluded. I allowed my cousin time to explain what he wanted to talk about. "Cuz I just wanna say I'm sorry about your sister. I never meant to get her shot. I didn't know what I was thinking at the time those bullets were ringing out. I was just trying to get away" said my cousin. After about ten minutes of explaining my cousin had the nerve to say that my sister shouldn't have been over there anyway. That was my breaking point and I completely lost it. I began to beat the life out of this boy once again. I swung him so many times that my arms became tired. He tried to run away but I made him trip over back foot and he tumbled and fell. As he fell I was able to straddle him and I began to choke him. I began to squeeze his neck until I felt no more movement. I went back to the time when my grandpa would train me in hand to hand contact. After two or three minutes his body just stopped moving and his eyes were huge. At this moment I knew I had killed my cousin. I instantly began to throw up. My stomach became so upset. It was true when they said that when you take a life your own body becomes sick and you begin to have flashes of the person (as if you could see dead people walking among the living).

    I began to think about my next steps and how I had to dispose of all the evidence, that would be step one. Step

A Hitman's Confessions

two, dispose of the body I couldn't afford to get caught for this and burn everything I had. I remembered these steps from watching the Goodfellas (which is my favorite movie). Step three get rid of all my clothes and anything that could tie me to the scene and step four, come up with an alibi. I had to find a place to be that could record my presence and give me the alibi I needed. I wasn't worried too much about my auntie and uncle wondering where he was and what had happened to him because he was a fuck up anyway. He wanted to be in the streets and was always around shooting at people plus after what happened to my sister and mom, no one really dealt with him not even his own parents. The sight of his lifeless body didn't bother me much because I had seen death more than a few times already so it didn't bother me looking and handling his body. I went to the Coney Island in the hood and sat there to have a bite to eat. I really wasn't hungry I only went there to be seen and to make sure my alibi was valid. I even made a scene to make sure the owner knew I was there. Gave him something to remember my presence. I began to think of what just happened and the feeling I got when I began to squeeze his neck. It felt natural to me, like I was used to it. I guess all those training days with my granddad made me a natural born killer at a young age and it took this kill to awaken a side of me I would have never known.

Chapter 5

My Skills Will Be Tested

It was October, around the end of me being sixteen years old. My birthday was next month and I would be turning seventeen. My uncle Charles that was in jail was recently release and would be staying at my Grandparents house until he is able to get himself together. My uncle Charles was a Vietnam veteran that served two terms in the jungles of Vietnam. He was shell shocked for sure, a clear case of PTSD. For those of you that don't know what PTSD is, it's Post-Traumatic Stress Disorder. He had it bad too. There were nights when he would wake up out of his sleep screaming and kicking and punching. Some nights we would catch him crawling through the hallways like he was still in the war. My granddad knew the signs of PTSD being a military guy himself so he knew what he was going through. I would be told stories about the war and how important it was for him to come home. People think that veterans who were in a war, only fight was against the enemy but that wasn't exactly true. There are many elements while in the jungle that were never talked about, like the bugs that would bite you and give you malaria and the swamp of water that they had to track through with leeches and fish that would nip at their ankles and last but not least the snakes and tigers that were in the jungle that would pop out at any time. They had to always stay alert and be prepared to face any battle that came their way. My uncle Charles just like myself was taught survival skills from my grandad as well. He told me that was the only reason he survived. The things he was taught in boot camp didn't prepare him but the skills he learned from grandad did. He also spoke on the friends he made and the people he watched die and the bodies he had to carry back to base. Not to mention the bodies that were completely mangled

A Hitman's Confessions

with cut off heads and blown off limbs. Like myself death didn't bother him much and I could relate.

Around this time the crack epidemic was big. With my mom still being in the streets it wasn't hard to find out who the big players were. Hell she would be around those guys daily. My mom was a beautiful lady and didn't look like the other women on drugs. She still managed to maintain her looks and her body was filled out nicely. My mom also still maintained her job and was making good money. Her only issued was that she still continued to use drugs to ease the pain of losing my little sister. My mom introduced my uncle to her supplier Big Rog. Big Rog was a drug dealer who had a lot of money and the flyest cars in the hood. Once my uncle starting dealing with Big Rog he started to see a lot of money. My uncle Charles was a super cocky dude and he was a killer, just what Big Rog needed. Before long my uncle Charles became the head of Big Rog security team and that's when all this shit started to get real.

A Hitman's Confessions

Right after my seventeenth birthday my uncle Charles came to me and asked me to ride with him somewhere. I was a little uneasy because I knew the reputation my uncle had in the streets. Since hooking up with Big Rog, multiple murders were committed and dozens of kidnappings. Uncle Charles gained the name of the Grim Reaper because if you saw him you were dead. So when he came to get me to ride with him I didn't know what to expect. We pulled up to this ranch style house that looked to be an upper class home. My uncle Charles got out of the car and started making a phone call. "I'm here and what's their names"? Uncle Charles said while on the phone. He was speaking low to avoid me hearing his conversation but I knew it was Big Rog on the other end. "Ok, ok, ok. I got it." Uncle Charles stated. I was told to sit in the car and watch his back. "Don't let nobody walk up on me Nephew, I mean nobody! If you see anyone coming there is a gun in the glove compartment you know what to do," said Uncle Charles.

A Hitman's Confessions

As much as I didn't want to be there with him it was a rush of excitement for me. After all I might get a chance to kill again and I was waiting for that opportunity. I grabbed the gun out of the glove compartment. It was a 45 caliber pistol with a lemon squeeze handle, fully loaded hollow tip round with a red laser beam on it. Needless to say it was an amazing weapon. I had wished I had one just like it or that I could hassle up enough nuts to ask my uncle for this one. Hell he had plenty of guns everywhere at the house I'm sure he wouldn't miss this one. Minutes later I heard five shots and shortly after saw my Uncle Charles running out of the house screaming! "Start the car and open the door now!" I did as instructed, while my uncle jumped in the car, speeding off. I asked him what the fuck was going on and what he did, even though I knew what the hell he did. "Look you don't know nothing you hear me?" said Uncle Charles while handing me an envelope full of money. I started counting the money it was $3500.

"Is this for me," I asked.

"Yeah, that's yours." Uncles Charles responded.

"For real?" I asked in shock.

"Yeah Lil' nigga for real." Uncle Charles stated as a matter of fact.

I made $3500 in ten minutes, I could do this all the time and that's when it started.

At this point I asked my uncle how I could continue to be a part.

"You not ready for this." Uncle Charles said.

"Yes I am, Grandad trained me too. I can handle this." I replied. That is when my skills were put to the test. Days later my uncle came to me and asked me a question.

"Are you ready Lil' nigga?

"Yeah I'm ready." I replied. We headed out, on the way to our destination and he tells me what the mission was while in the car. Once we arrived at the destination he asked me again.

"You sure you're ready?"

"Yeah I'm ready. Why you keep asking me that? I told you I'm ready."

My Uncle Charles then explained to me what he needed done.

"Listen this is what I need you to do. We are going to go in there and the first person you see, I want you to shoot him in the head. Right in the head, you got me?" said my Uncle Charles while looking me dead in the eyes.

"Yeah, I got you." I replied.

This was a little different from hunting deer, so my nerves were jumping but I didn't say anything. My Uncle Charles reached in the glove box and handed me that same 45 I had seen before. We pulled up to a house and he stopped the car and we both proceeded to get out. We approached the front door of the house and my uncle knocks on the door as if we were some Jehovah witnesses or something. Seconds later someone answered the door.

A Hitman's Confessions

"Hello Sir, we are here from the temple of the Lord, can we speak to you?" States my Uncle Charles. The man says no and started to close the door but before he could close the door, my uncle rushed in and grabbed the man by his neck. "Shoot him!" my Uncle Charles yelled. I paused for a minute cause my heart was pumping. "Shoot him now!" My Uncle Charles said again. I was afraid of what my uncle might do to me for freezing up so I shot the man. Bang the gun went!

I couldn't believe I had just shot a man for no reason. I wanted to run but I had to prove to my Uncle Charles that I was ready. As I watched the man's brains hit the floor, things once again felt like Deja Vu and I became nauseous and almost lost my lunch.

"You bet not throw up in here boy!" I heard my uncle yell at me as he let the body hit the floor. "Now let's go through this house and shoot everything in here moving, you hear me?" said Uncle Charles.

A Hitman's Confessions

"Yeah Unk, I hear you." I replied.

We proceeded to go through house looking for people. I was hoping no one else was in there, seeing as how I was already shaken from the first kill. Shooting a person was completely different than shooting an animal. True you are taking the life of a living creature either way but a human being who was just like you, walking and talking, was a different story. Killing a human being was like taking someone's power from them, it was a completely different feeling altogether. After looking in every room and every closet in this man's house I was happy to find that there was no one else there. I returned to where my uncle was and found that he had dismantled the man's body with a kitchen knife and puts the remains inside of a garbage bag. My Uncle Charles threw the big black bag over his shoulder and headed towards the door, gesturing that it was time to leave. Once we got to the car, my Uncle Charles popped the trunk opened and threw the bag into the trunk. Once he was done with that we got inside the car and drove off. As we were driving he was trying to make small talk with me and then afterwards he handed me an envelope again. "You almost froze up on me huh?" My Uncle Charles stated. I just looked at him, denying it like I wasn't shook in that moment for killing that man. Honestly, now that we were in the car and away from the scene I didn't feel anything. I was actually calm now. Again I looked inside the envelope to find that my uncle had now given me $5000, even more than the last time.

"What's' this Unk?" I said.

"That's for you Lil' nigga. You did great. You're better than I thought you were." Uncle Charles said. From that day on I was his right hand man and his soldier.

Chapter 6

Seasoned Veteran

Months have gone by and I have had many more encounters with my uncle. I was sitting on some serious money. I gave my grandmother money to make sure she was ok. She kept asking me where I was getting this money from and I would often lie to her to keep her off track of what I was really doing. Everyone knew I was making money but couldn't tell where it was coming from. My cousin Louie Percheise finally came to me and asked. "What's up Cuz, you keeping secrets from me? What's good?" Lou was a soldier in his own right. He grew up in another part of town than me. He was raised in HP. In Highland Park there was a lot of killers and hustlers. Lou was a year older than me but grandpa had taught him all the same things he had taught me, only difference was Lou didn't stay with us every day. Lou would only come over on some weekends. Needless to say, he was one of my favorite cousins. I decided if I was going to continue with this lifestyle I was going to need a team. My cousin Lou, his brother Rob and their partner Jay. Louie was a monster in the streets already and so was Rob. They were the dynamic duo of Hp. Jay was a Lil' nigga. I was kind of concerned about him but I got the chance to see him in action. Plus my cuz gave me his validation so I decided to run with him as well.

  I organized a meeting to finally reveal to them what I was doing. I knew I was taking a chance revealing this information but Lou was my guy and I knew he would understand. I also knew he would keep everything quiet but I was concerned about Rob and Jay. I started the meeting off saying, "What I'm about to tell y'all can't be repeated to a soul." After everyone agreed I proceeded to talk to them about what I was doing and what my plans were with them.

A Hitman's Confessions

As I told them what was going on their mouths dropped opened and I had their full attention. I make $5000 a lick and I need a team to help me because this is becoming too much for me to handle by myself. When they heard the price they were all in but before I could just trust them I had to put them in a situation to test their loyalty and for me to also get dirt on them. I told them what my Uncle Charles and I was putting together and they was excited. I had thought ahead and figured my Uncle Charles could continue to dictate and get the jobs and my team and I could be the ones to pull the jobs off. Uncle Charles knew about his nephews Lou and Rob but he wasn't too sure about Jay. I asked my uncle to arrange a job, advising that this would be their test and the dirt I needed to get on them. I told my Uncle this job would be a way to ensure that no one would flip on me for the information I told them prior. Like clockwork my uncle came through an hour later. My uncle Charles wanted us to hit this house where these

A Hitman's Confessions

Asians lived. They were a weight house for a rival kingpin that my uncle had a problem with. My uncle wasn't concerned about retaliation he was actually hoping the guy would retaliate. I explained the mission to our team and everyone was down with it, so we headed to do the job.

As we approach the house we saw the Asian chicks pulling up to the crib as we pulled down the street. "Ok look, we are going to go in there and kill everyone! No one lives." Stated my Uncle Charles. The same speech my uncle had given me on my first job, is the same one he was giving them. No one lives was our saying. We couldn't risk having witnesses. Witnesses would get you caught and even though what I was doing was in fact wrong, I still didn't want to go to jail. We got to the house, guns out and ready. Rob kicked in the door as Lou, Jay and myself rushed into the house. "Go all through this bitch and round up everybody." Uncle Charles said. So we scattered throughout the house gathering up everybody and brought them all to the living room. We began tying up everyone. There were two grown Asians and a young woman who looked to be about 25 years old. Once everyone was tied up I began to ask where all the work and money was. No one answered. The two Asians were acting tough. This was a situation I've encounter many of times with my uncle, people trying to hold out and we would have to beat or torture them until they talked. I was surprised at how the guys were handling the situation. It was looking like I picked the right team.

    It was time to step our game up and get these people talking. I had Lou beat the older Asian and Rob beat the other one. Then I had Jay beat the young lady. Jay had an issue with the duties given and was conflicted until I made him get it together. I had to remind him that this was his introduction into the life and if he couldn't handle it he would have to die right along with them. Not that he wasn't my guy but I couldn't afford for him to live knowing what we were into. Lou and Rob didn't hesitate they went right to business as if they've done this before. After about an hour or so of torture they finally gave up where the drugs and money were. We grabbed all the work and money. Now we had to get rid of the witnesses. There were three lives that had to be taken. That meant that each one of the guys on my team had to have a body. Lou was the first to shoot his victim and Rob followed suit but Jay was having issues with pulling the trigger. Jay couldn't bring himself to do it. Jay stood over the girl's body and had the gun pointed on her but just couldn't take her life. Lou witness the hesitation in his boy and tried to convince him to do it. "Jay you gotta do this. Come on man!" Lou yelled. Jay said nothing and continued to stand there like he was frozen, so I took it upon myself to finish the job. I took a pillow off the sofa and place it on the young lady's head and shot through the pillow. Then I turned around and shot Jay dead in the face.

Jay body dropped to the ground and I looked towards the others and motioned to them that it was time to go. We left the house and the ride back in the car was quiet. Lou and Rob finally broke the silence.

"Well you did tell the Lil' nigga. Oh well, I guess this was our test huh?" Rob said.

"Yeah it was a test and I had to have dirt on you guys so you couldn't flip on me. Plus I needed to know if y'all could handle yourselves, which y'all passed with flying colors, except for that Lil' nigga Jay. So can you handle doing this on a regular basis because if so we are all going to get paid?" I said.

They both agreed so we returned back to where Unk was and handed him the bags we got from the house. My Uncle Charles looked inside and threw us back the bag that had the cash in it. "This is for y'all." He said. Inside the bag was a shit load of cash. We all began to count the money up. There was about 55,000 dollars in that bag which was more than I've ever taken in on one job alone. We split cash and that gave us each 18,333 dollars. Lou and Rob were excited.

"Is this the kind of money we can make on the regular?" asked Lou.

"Yes it is. So again, so that I'm clear are y'all in or out?" I asked while looking at them both, awaiting their answer.

"Hell yeah we in!" They yelled together.

After a few months Lou, Rob and I had pulled off numerous jobs. This was in the 90's in Detroit when the city drug kingpins were fighting for territory throughout the city. Big Rog and his partners began to fall out with each other over what I wasn't sure about but it put my uncle in a weird place. Seeing as how he was head of security for the whole organization. My Uncle became torn on which side he should take as he was loyal to all of them. When it was all said and done my Uncle decided to stay with Big Rog.

A Hitman's Confessions

My uncle knew that the beef was sure to come but he was worried about the fact that the whole organization knew he was a certified killer and he wasn't sure if after choosing a side if the others would turn on him. My uncle was ready for whatever so he called us in for a meeting to inform us of what could come. The plan was for us all to chill for a while until things were figured out. My uncle was also worried about my Grandparents house and close family members and the others who he was no longer riding for coming after them. My uncle knew when beef comes there were no rules. Everyone can become a victim, even though my granddad was a motherfucker himself but he was getting older so it was important for us to watch over them. We had pulled dozens of jobs in the city and the beef could come from anywhere.

A Hitman's Confessions

Chapter 7

When Shit Hits the Fan

It took months for the streets to settle down. As you can imagine there was plenty of bloodshed. Instead of dealers taking over blocks they were taking over complete sides of town. The kingpins decided to hold out on selling drugs to the street level guys and started their own little corner hustles that pushed the middle and lower level guys out and it was easy to take over their areas. When this happened the middle and lower guys began robbing and killing everything they could to survive. I see now why my uncle told us to chill because the streets became way too hot to still be putting in work. Then things turned for the worst. My uncle boss man wounded up getting killed. He went to open his car wash like he always did and then he was ambushed and shot in the head. The bad part about it is

A Hitman's Confessions

that my uncle was supposed to be with him but he had to check on his baby girl she had fell down some steps and broke her arm. The coincidence is Big Rog was brought to the same hospital that my uncle was in with his daughter. See Big Rog didn't die instantly he was still hanging on to life but he was unconscious. As they rolled Big Rog into the emergency room they passed by my uncle and that's how he found out. When my uncle seen Big Rog being wheeled in he went crazy right there in the hospital.

One of the neighbors had called the police and ambulance and rode to the emergency room with Big Rog just in case he needed to tell the police what had happen. The neighbor that rode with Big Rog was able to tell the police everything because the cameras on the side of his house caught everything. After the guy was finished talking to the police. My uncle approached him and commanded he tell him what he told the police. The man was caught by surprise and didn't want to tell my uncle anything. At-least, until my uncle made it clear that if he didn't tell him that he wouldn't make it home that day. My uncle informed the guy that Big Rog was his boss and he needed to find out what had happened. The guy told my uncle that there was a tape of what happened but he had to turn it in to the cops. My uncle demanded to see it before he turned it over to the police. My uncle told his daughter's mother he would be back he had to go review this tape before the police got a hold of it. He offered the man some cash and the guy accepted the money and they left to view the tape. When they arrive to the guy's house he loaded the footage onto his computer. As it downloaded my uncle was impatiently waiting.

"How long is this going to take?" Uncle Charles asked.

"Just a few more seconds." The neighbor responded.

A Hitman's Confessions

When the download was completed the guy showed my uncle the footage. It showed Big Rog getting out his truck and walking up to the door to open the car wash. Seconds later a black Lexus GT coupe pulls up and begins shooting out of the passenger side window. My uncle became so furious because he knew exactly whose car it was. My uncle never told the guy what he knew he just said thank you to the guy and left.

Afterwards my uncle came to my Grandparents house to grab his guns and vest and few things that was in his stash at their house so the cops couldn't find them. Even though he had his own crib he would put things at their house. Once Uncle Charles loaded up all the weapons he was taken, he put on his bullet proof vest and grabbed his knives. While he was getting prepared I asked him did he need me to go with him. "No nephew I got this one," he replied. I knew he had to be upset because he called me nephew, normally he called me Lil' nigga. He said it so

A Hitman's Confessions

much that I thought that was my name. In the game we are in, you can't have emotions. Emotions make you sloppy and reckless. I knew he was on a mission of vengeance. The person that killed Big Rog was in fact his older brother. His older brother was always jealous of the money and power his brother had. He use to work for his brother but got cut off because he was always a liability. The brother always had an excuse for when shit went wrong and he was always getting robbed. When the fact was he was just lying and keeping the money. This is what made my uncle so furious because he wanted to kill him years ago but didn't because Big Rig would always stop him but this time it was war.

    My uncle Charles left the house on his way to go search for Big Rog brother. After days of sitting and waiting at Big Rog brother house, Big Rog brother had finally returned to his crib. I guess he figured it was safe to return because no one was talking about the murder of Big

A Hitman's Confessions

Rog. The police just chalked it up to a drug deal gone bad seeing as how there were drugs at the car wash which explained why Big Rog was there. My uncle was really bothered about this one. Although he was a stone cold killer he had grown fawned of Big Rog after spending so much time with the guy. Now that Big Rog brother was home it's time for his life to end for what he had done to Big Rog. My uncle bust through the door like Rambo, gun blazing wild and reckless. This was not his style. My uncle was usually very professional but with his emotions running wild he was not on point as usually. Big Rog's brother was in fact on the couch when my uncle came in and caught 4 bullets to the chest. He was lying slumped over on the couch and died after the first bullet which hit him directly in the heart.

    My uncle stood and starred at the lifeless body with a feeling of relief, knowing that he had conquered his goal. As my uncle turned to walk out the door, he was shot in his

A Hitman's Confessions

head. My uncle didn't canvas the house like he usually did and ended up getting caught slipping. My uncle always taught us to leave no witnesses and search the whole house to make sure no one else was there but on this day his emotions took over. After a couple weeks it was time to lay my uncle to rest. Surprisingly, there were a lot of people who showed up to pay their respects to my uncle. The amount of people that attended my uncle funeral was crazy. I didn't know how many people truly rocked with that crazy man. My uncle was a killer and was feared by many which I knew but he had to be living a double life. The praises he received from his former army brothers and friends, showed me a side of my uncle Charles that I never knew. The stories they shared were like he was in the room telling me them himself. I was reminded of how much I would miss my uncle Charles but I also knew that the game we were in was bound to catch up with us.

A Hitman's Confessions

After the death of Big Rog and my uncle Charles I figured my career was over. My duty now was to make sure my mom got the help she needed. It was time to put my family structure back together because we had already took too many loses. My mom deserved to be back to where she was before all this happened. I spoke with my mom about getting her some help and she agreed to go to rehab. I promised her that if she completed rehab I would make sure she had the money she needed to live comfortably. After a couple of months in rehab, my mom was released and back to being the mother I once knew. As promised on the day of her completion of rehab, I handed her 125,000 dollars in cash. My mom broke down and cried tears of joy. I always wanted my mom back to person she was when I was a young child. When everything made sense and to see being the woman I always knew, made life beautiful, even if it was only for a moment.

Chapter 8

Getting Back to Me

After the passing of my uncle and my mother being released from rehab, I was back to being a normal teenager. Which was fine for me but I was missing the thrill. I had also run out of money due to giving my mom all the money that I had saved up. I was considering getting back into the game. In fact, Lou and I talked about it all the time. I knew my cousins and I were a great team. I would go to the gun range just to shoot and keep my aim precise. When my uncle passed I was left with all his weapons, seeing as how nobody but me knew where he was keeping them. That 45 caliber I always admired was finally mines. I was frequently visiting this one gun range across 8 mile where my uncle and I use to go to all the time. The owner knew me and my uncle Charles, so although I was under age he would let me shoot at his range with no problem. While shooting at the range I was approached by this older white man who was shooting in the corner, not too far away from me.

"Great skills young man. I was watching you shoot from over there. You have a very great aim. Where did you learn?"

"My grandfather taught how to hunt as a young man." I replied.

"What kind of weapon are you shooting?" The older white man asked me.

"Oh this is a 45 Remington with a laser sight." I stated.

"What kind of weapons can you handle young man?"

"I can handle any weapon you put in front of me." I replied as a matter of fact.

"Yeah right! If you so sure, shoot this." The older white man said while handing me an AA12 shotgun with a 50 round drum on it. "Only professionals can handle this." The older white man said.

What he didn't know was that I was in fact a professional and was taught to handle any gun. Once I started shooting the AA12 I was not only handling the weapon but I was also very accurate with my shots.

"Wow young man, where are you from? Your granddad taught you very well." The older white man said stunned.

"Yeah I love shooting. It calms me. I also like the sound and being able to hit a target precise." I stated.

We talked for hours about guns, shooting and gun maintenance. It was amazing how much we had in common. The man was very impressed by the knowledge I had as a young man and how much I knew about things way beyond my age group. The older white man asked if it

A Hitman's Confessions

was possible for him to call me or get in touch with me in the near future. He claimed he wanted to show me his gun magazine. We exchanged numbers and contact info and then he left. I continued shooting my gun when the owner approached me and asked what the older white man and I was speaking about. I told him we were just talking about guns and then he told me to be careful with that guy because he was a bad man. The owner really didn't get into much detail but he did in fact warn me about the man. I thanked him for the information and I packed up to leave. As I was leaving, the owner warned me again about the older white man. I started to ask why he was warning me but I figured he didn't want me to know or else he would have told me. The relationship the owner had with my uncle made him feel like he had to at-least warn me without saying too much. Regardless to the warning I received I still decided to reach out to the man.

A Hitman's Confessions

We talked briefly and made a decision to meet up at the Coney Island to have lunch and continue talking. While we were having lunch the conversation came up about work and what my plans were for the future. I really didn't have an answer. All I ever knew how to do was shoot and kill. My grandad tried to gear me towards the military like himself and all my uncles but I never wanted to go. I told the guy I didn't have an answer for that because I never learned to do anything. He informed me that he owned a gun store and I could possibly work for him seeing as how I had vast knowledge of guns and weapons. This was right up my alley. I could work with guns and have a chance to touch and feel all the weapons I was thrilled about. This couldn't be true. I couldn't help but think why the owner of the gun range Sam warned me about this dude. I soon found out that the man name's was Tim Reed. Tim Reed was an old white man with a cane but was able to shoot the shit out of any weapon even at his old age. Tim took a

A Hitman's Confessions

liking to me the first time he met me. I accepted the job offer seeing as though my mom had all the money I had saved and she was in fact doing well because of it, so I couldn't complain. My mom never asked about the money. She knew I was running errands for my uncle but she didn't know what and decided to leave well enough alone.

    It wasn't long before I began working for Tim and to be honest working for Tim was fun as hell! This guy knew how to treat his employees and everything was going smooth. I still couldn't understand why Sam had warned me about Tim. Until one day Tim asked me if I wanted to make some extra money. I was confused because Tim was paying me well to work at the gun store. I wondered what he needed me to do for this extra cash, not that it mattered because I was always about my money as long as it wasn't some freak nasty shit I was good. Tim had me meet him at the Motor City Casino parking structure to discuss what he had in mind. I wasn't old enough to get into the casino so meeting him there had me concerned.

"Ok Colt are you ready for some real work?" Tim asked.

"Real work. What do you mean Tim? What are we doing here?" I asked a little puzzled. "There is something I never talked to you about. I'm a hitman for hire." Tim said blankly.

"A hitman, really?" I responded.

"Yeah really. I am a hitman but I'm getting older and I'm looking for a replacement so I can retire." Tim said.

I couldn't believe this older white man was a hitman. It was all starting to make sense now. The knowledge of guns, him owning a gun store and him being at the shooting range daily. Wow this was mind blowing. All the time he spent talking and hanging out with me, was him grooming me to take his position. Tim popped the trunk and pulled out a sniper rifle with a scope on it so big you could see it well across town. The spot Tim picked in this parking structure was very dark and hidden off in a corner with no cameras or customers coming to gamble. Tim had a black Mat with a tripod for the gun already set up and ready to go. This was my test to see if I could kill. What he didn't know was that my whole teen life was spent murdering and killing. I failed to mention my past due to being shocked from the news he told me.

"I have placed a watermelon 300 feet away. I need to know if you can hit a target precise from long distances." Tim said.

"I could do this with my eyes closed." I replied to Tim.

This reminded me of the days I was hunting with my granddad. I kept telling myself…keep calm, breath slow and then squeeze. Perfect! Tim looked at me amazed at what he had just witnessed.

A Hitman's Confessions

"You are just what I'm looking for. Do you understand that's 300 feet away? It's not too many people that can handle that type of shot. You are amazing!" Tim stated smiling. Tim was in awe of me. He praised me constantly. "I can make you rich young man. Do you want to be rich?" Tim asked.

"Hell yeah I want to be rich Tim. What kind of question is that?" I replied.

"Do you think you can kill a person?" Tim asked no longer smiling.

"Tim I have something to tell you. I have been killing people since I was sixteen years old. I worked as a hitman for my uncle who passed away some months ago." I stated.

"What! You have got to be killing me! Who was your uncle?" Tim asked.

"Charles Washington. He used to go to the gun range we was at too." I responded. Tim looked at me with a puzzled face.

"Are you serious Charles was your uncle?" Tim questioned.

"Yes. Charles was my uncle. Did you know him?" I asked surprised.

"Yes I knew him. Your uncle use to work for me. He was a good man until he let his emotions get to him." Tim stated as he turned his head in disappointment.

"What? What the hell are you talking about Tim? How did he work for you when he was working for Big Rog? I know that for a fact because I use to pull jobs with him." I paused for a minute, not believing what I was hearing. "So when I was pulling all those jobs for my uncle he was working for you?" I asked in disbelief.

A Hitman's Confessions

"Yes I was the contact for those jobs. This explains why you can shoot so well. You were taught by the best. I know your family history." Tim said.

I was in a state of shock. All of this was mind blowing. There was a brief moment of silence and then Tim reached for his gun and put it directly to my head.

"What about to tell you now will determine whether you live or die. I killed your uncle." Tim stated.

"What the fuck are you talking about? My uncle got killed taking revenge for his old boss, I mean homeboy Big Rog." I said confused.

"Yeah I know that but what you didn't know was that I put the hit out on Big Rog and your uncle knew all about it. Why do you think he wasn't with him the day he was killed at the car wash? Your uncle was supposed to do the hit himself. He was paid very well for that job but instead he had someone else pull it off. That's why he's dead. I found out that he got Big Rog brother to pull the hit off for him and then he killed Big Rog brother to cover his own tracks." Tim explained while still holding the gun to my head. I couldn't believe what I was hearing. *Was this man capping or was he really just telling me that my uncle was responsible for killing his own friend?* I thought to myself.

"What the fuck is going on here?" I asked still confused. Then it all started to make sense once he started explaining things in more details. "What about the guy at the hospital with the tape. The neighbor?" I asked Tim.

"Yeah Jimmy. That's my guy. I wanted proof that Big Rog was dead and the people that employed us wanted footage of the actual killing, that's why it was recorded. Your uncle took the tape from Jimmy, once again trying to cover his own tracks but what he didn't know was that Jimmy and I followed him. When he killed Big Rog brother we was there waiting and I shot him in the head." Tim said.

"WOW this is too much. So my uncle died because he didn't go through with a hit he was paid to do?" I asked baffled.

"Yeah. That's why he died. He was paid to kill and did not complete the mission. In this game that warrants death and he was fully aware of the circumstances." Tim stated as a matter of fact.

After hearing all this I was totally confused. Now I knew what Sam meant when he told me to be careful dealing with Tim. Sam was warning me because he knew that Tim was the man my uncle was working for and I wouldn't be surprise if Sam knew that Tim was the one responsible for killing my uncle.

"So what's it going to be young buck life or death?" Tim asked me.

"Life." I answered.

"I'm going to put this pistol away but if you ever try and test me I'm going to bury you I promise." Tim replied as he tucked the gun under his shirt. "Now let's get down to business. I want you to be my go to guy. I don't want you kicking in doors and all that silly shit. I only want you to do special hits. High profile type stuff shit. Not like your uncle. He was a loose cannon and being in the war really fucked him up." Tim stated. I had to agree with that statement. My uncle was fucked up in the head for sure.

"I want you to be a paid assassin. Like I said before I can make you rich. Are you ready or not?" Tim questioned while looking at me directly in the eyes.

"Yes I'm ready." I responded even though I was upset about the information I found out about my uncle, I knew I had to put my feelings aside and play the game.

Chapter 9

Back to Business

Tim called me and told me he needed to see me. I met him for lunch like we've done dozens of times this time he had a job for me. This would be my first job for him and I didn't know what to expect. Tim pulled out this computer with pictures of a man and began to describe what he needed done.

"I want you to put a bullet right in the middle of his head not in the neck or chest but the head." Tim directed.

"Yes sir where do you want me to go? Where's the house at?" I asked.

"House? Who said anything about a house? I didn't say anything about a house. He has an office. I want you to take the shot as he is walking to his car. You will be station three buildings away. He has a gold BMW 745. You have to be ready because he moves very fast. He moves like a ghost. You see him then you don't. This is a very big mark his head pays $100,000 to my employer." Tim explained thoroughly.

"Bet! How soon do you want this done?" I asked excited.

"Immediately. This has to be done sooner than later." Tim stated.

"Ok, well I'm out." I stated as I made my exit, preparing to handle this mission.

I set up my place to get ready to take this shot. This was a lot different from brute force take overs. You have to be precise every time no mistakes. I laid down and got into position and arranged my scope. I fixed it on the driver side of the BMW and begin waiting. Just like Tim said he left his office building at exactly 3:45pm. He looked around before walking towards his car. I prepared to take the shot right as he grabbed his door handle I shot. Bang! The gun

A Hitman's Confessions

went. I sent a direct shot right to his head. I saw his brain shoot out the other side of his head through the scope. *Mission accomplished!* I said to myself. I got in touch with Tim right after and arranged for us to meet up at the Coney we always met at. Once I was there we begin talking about the mission.

"Mission accomplished. I did it exactly as you requested. A direct headshot." I told Tim.

"I know I was watching. I saw it for myself." Tim responded as he took a sip of his water.

"Huh? What do you mean you were watching?" I asked surprised. Tim took another sip of his water and calmly responded.

"One thing I will tell you about myself is that I'm always watching." Tim said while looking me directly in the eyes. "Here you go, great job young buck." Tim said while handing me a duffel bag.

A Hitman's Confessions

It was a duffel bag full of money. I would have had to pull dozens of jobs for my uncle to get this kind of cash but I pulled one job and got all this. I was thinking to myself I couldn't wait for the next job. Everything seemed to going good. I was finally back in my bag and making more money than I ever made. On top of that my mother was also still doing well. My mother had used the money I had given her after rehab to invest in herself. By this time my mom had started her own business and opened up a real estate office. Real Estate was a perfect way to invest this money I was making. I promised my mom she would get back to where she should be if it killed me. My mom was used to dating hustlers so the amount of money I started give her to invest in some properties didn't take her by surprise. My mom figured I was into something but she just didn't know exactly what and to be honest I don't think she really cared. As long as she was happy so was I.

A Hitman's Confessions

A few months had past and Tim once again contacted me to meet up. "What's up young buck? I got another job for you. This time it's a little more high profile. It's a government official who will have lots of security. Do you think you can handle this mission? There's a very slim chance of escape but well worth the risk." Tim cautioned. I sat there for a moment contemplating on what Tim had just said and ask myself was it worth it. Then I thought about how much money I made from the last mission and figured why the hell not.

"What are we talking about Tim? How much money are we talking?" I asked ready to get to the point. Tim glanced around making sure no one was listening.

"A million dollars. You think you could do it?" Tim asked as a matter fact.

All I could think about was how my life could be set. *A million dollars! A million dollars!* I thought to myself. Is this nigga for real? Who the fuck did he want me

A Hitman's Confessions

to kill? The fucking president or something, I wondered. I asked Tim who the target would be.

"Well it's the mayor of Detroit City. I have a partner who invested in his demise and is willing to pay handsomely for this kill. So what do you say young buck can you handle this mission?"

I thought for a second how hard it would be to get a good shot especially with the mayor have so much security. The money sounded real good but it was going to be a lot to do.

"Do I have time to answer? I need to scope out the layout and pick the right weapon etc." I explained.

"No not really. I already told him you would do it and it goes down tomorrow. There will be a grand opening of the new casino and there is where it will need to happen. The mayor will be giving a speech and while he is giving his speech is when I need you to take the shot." Tim stated assuming I would say yes.

A Hitman's Confessions

I was taken aback and was kind of furious that Tim made a decision on my behalf without consulting me first. Yes this would be a game changer but my life was also on the line. A hit on someone that is high profile takes preparation and planning and that couldn't be done in one day. I needed to learn how the mayor moved and to see exactly how many security guards he kept around. This was a big decision and one that I wasn't happy Tim made alone.

"You already made a decision for me? How are you just going to make a decision without...?" I was saying but before I could finish my sentence Tim cut me off.

"You work for me! I say what you do and don't do." Tim said with authority. I was shock at how Tim was coming at me.

"What do you mean Tim I work for you? You don't own me." I said back with just as much authority.

A Hitman's Confessions

"You do what I say you do. Don't forget what happened to your uncle for catching feelings. The same can happen to you." Tim stated.

I knew this was a dangerous game I was playing and every time Tim mentioned my uncle I got a funny feeling. I really wanted to kill Tim for that bullshit but he is getting me paid. I started contemplating on the options I had. I could take this last job and let this be my way out and if I choose not to Tim would for sure kill me. I could already see it. I didn't have a choice, so I agreed to do the job.

"Okay Tim I will do it. When and where? Do you have the specs on the job?" I asked unenthused.

"Here's half up front. You will get the other half after the job is done." Tim said while handing me another duffel bag full of cash. "See you tomorrow and don't forget I will be watching." Tim said while walking away.

A Hitman's Confessions

I had really gotten myself in too deep and the fact that Tim had to remind me that he would be watching, made me uneasy. At any time Tim could take me out. I had to figure out an escape plan and be done with this life once and for all.

A Hitman's Confessions

Chapter 10

The End All Be All

    I arrived to the spot where I was to take position for the hit on the mayor I getting ready to do. I arrived a little earlier than expected so that I could take the proper steps to ensure a good getaway. Seeing as how it was a lot of security everywhere, I had to blend in with the crowd in order to get away clean. I had to use a long range sniper rifle that was easy to break down and pack away without being notice. After doing my surveillance of the area. I got into position and was ready. I fixed my sights on the microphone stand in which the mayor would be speaking. I knew Tim would be watching me from somewhere but I didn't know where. As the mayor was approaching the stage I started to get nervous, just as I did with my first kill. I was hunting all over again. It's true that every time you

A Hitman's Confessions

kill you always recall the very first time. This kill however felt different than the others, something just didn't feel right but I got myself ready.

The mayor began his speech and I closed my eyes and took a deep breath and open them back up and shot. Bang! I sent a shot right through the mayor head, right between his eyes. I watched his security scramble trying to find out where the shot came from. Then I heard other shots coming from another direction. Bang! Bang! The shots went. The security converted their attention to the second set of shots that were heard. This allowed me the chance to pack up and leave with the scurry of traffic. I blended in with the crowd rushing to get away from the scene and then I received a call. It was Lou my cousin. "It's done cuzzo. We got him but I don't think Robs going to make it." Lou said panicking. You see I knew I had to get Tim's ass so I called my cousins and had them set up on Tim. Watch the watcher is what I told myself. I knew Tim was so fixed on me completing this job that he wouldn't expect what was coming. Plus when I told my cousins what happened to Uncle Charles they were all for it. This ensured my way out. Now I could go on with my life without worrying about Tim bastard ass putting a bullet in my brain at any moment.

    For months following the mayor's death things in the city became very hectic and the police were combing the streets looking for answers. Since Tim was dead I went back and ran the gun store. Tim didn't have any children of his own or family that I knew off so it was no problem for me to take over. Everyone already knew I was an employee there and it was like nothing had ever happened. When people ask for Tim I would just tell them he was out running errands and would be back shortly. One day a well dress white man came into the gun store asking for Tim and said that he had to speak to him and that it was an urgent matter. I informed him that Tim was out of town and

A Hitman's Confessions

wouldn't be back any time soon. The man had been in the store before so he knew I was super close to Tim.

"I have a package for him. Can I leave it with you?" The man asked.

"Sure. You can leave it with me and I will make sure Tim gets it." I responded as I retrieve the bag from the man. It was a duffel bag like Tim would always give me. I knew it was the rest of that payment I was owed for that job with the mayor. "I will definitely make sure he receives it." I ensured the man knowing all along I was going to keep the bag. I called Lou and told him to meet me at the Coney Island that Tim and I would always meet at. Rob had gotten caught trying to get away from the scene. They were trying to pin the mayor's murder on him but didn't have any evidence to convict him. We paid for Rob lawyer and we weren't worried about him. We knew he would be getting out, it was just a matter of time before he did.

A Hitman's Confessions

Lou met with me and we began talking about what had happened with the guy coming in the store with the money. We ordered our food and began eating. Lou looked up and started to say something to me but before Lou could finish his sentence, his head fell right into his food. *What the fuck?* I thought to myself. I looked around for some kind of assistance. I just thought he had passed out because there was no blood splatter plus where the fuck could this shot had come from. The windows were bullet proof, which was why Tim like to meet here. I screamed for the guy behind the counter to call for help. Just then my vision became blurry. I was getting dizzy…*what the fuck?* I thought to myself once again. Come to find out the cooks had poisoned us.

"Man, what the fuck did you give us you fuckers?" I said barely able to speak.

Then all of a sudden Tim appeared from behind the counter.

A Hitman's Confessions

"Surprise! You little niggas thought you had me didn't you? You thought you were smart huh? I saw them through my scope way before they set up on me. You got some amateurs to take me out, you ignorant bastard! I was the one that sent that gentleman into the gun shop with the cash. I've been tracking your every step, waiting for the perfect time to take you both out. Now it's your turn to die." Tim said angrily as he pulled out his pistol.

I was still in a dizzy state barely able to move and I couldn't protect myself. Everything I had done was finally catching up with me and all I could think was. *Is this how it ends a bullet to the head? I guess so this is the life I chose.* BANG! BANG! The gun went and just like that YOU'RE DEAD!!!!!!

About the Author

Yuanis grew up on the west side of Detroit during the height of the crack era but now resides in Georgia. This story is a huge part of Yuanis up-bringing. At 36 years old Yuanis suffered a heart attack that caused him to lose his kidneys and during that time, while on dialysis, Yuanis ran into one of the most notorious hitman's of Detroit during the 90s. This man whom we will call Anonymous discussed many trying times during that era which prompted Yuanis to write this book. After Yuanis received his kidney transplant he felt lead to publish this manuscript about the most notorious hitman after he passed away on his dialysis chair. As Yuanis continues to embark on his new found gift as a writer, you can be certain that there will be more to come!

Author Contact: yheathington@yahoo.com

Book Cover Design By: Anthony Temple

Made in the USA
Columbia, SC
20 March 2024